TROLLS, ELVES
and
FAIRIES
Coloring Book

JAN SOVAK

DOVER PUBLICATIONS, INC.
Mineola, New York

Bibliographical Note

Trolls, Elves and Fairies Coloring Book is a new work, first published by
Dover Publications, Inc., in 2002.

International Standard Book Number

ISBN-13: 978-0-486-42382-1
ISBN-10: 0-486-42382-4

Manufactured in the United States by Courier Corporation
42382410   2015
www.doverpublications.com

1. Alberich

Alberich is king of all dwarfs. He's not good looking, but he lives splendidly
in a great underground castle full of marvelous treasures. He is keeper of a
magical ring, a cloak of invisibility, and a sword with special powers.

2. Raviyoyla

The gentle fairy Raviyoyla knows about the healing properties of every single plant and flower in the world. She likes to help sick people, and is especially fond of small children.

3. Dwarfs

We all know a little bit about dwarfs. But very few people know that they are really goblins with magical powers. This lets them change how they look, or change their shape—or even become invisible! Dwarfs are the guardians of great treasures such as jewels or precious metals.

4. Puddlefoot

This funny-looking brownie—who might live secretly in your home—has some housekeeping habits that take some getting used to. Before he shows up at night, he loves to splash and swim in nearby ponds and puddles. So if you come home late, you'll see his tiny footprints everywhere. It's true that he makes a mess of what had been clean and tidy—but he makes up for that by cleaning up all messy things.

5. Mermaids

Stories about these beautiful young maidens with fish tails exist in folklore all over the world. Sometimes they marry humans, but almost always return to their underwater home. If you were ever to help a mermaid in distress—like rescuing her from a beach after a storm—she would offer you incredible gifts . . . or even a cure for a fatal disease!

6. Sandman

Sandman—sometimes called "Dustman"—is a nursery spirit who helps small
children fall asleep. He comes by in the evening to sprinkle magical sand or dust
above their beds. *(Shhh! Don't make a sound! Here he comes!)*

7. Trolls

There are bad trolls and good trolls. The bad ones are big, hairy, and not very smart—like this bewildered fellow in the picture. A good troll is more like a dwarf: if he likes you, he'll help you any way he can, even to the point of catching any bad troll that annoys you. Good trolls can also do all of the hard work around your house—after special training, of course.

8. Ana

In gypsy fairy tales, the splendid Ana is Queen of All Fairies. She is pure and beautiful and always ready to help humans. Ana lives high in the mountains in a great castle.

9. Cloud People

Native North Americans who make their pueblo homes in the southwestern deserts need rain for drinking water and to make things grow on their parched land. To help them, the good Cloud People look down from their abodes in the sky and bring rain to those who deserve this precious gift.

10. Goblins

Like their cousins the friendly brownies, goblins live in borrowed houses, right there (but well hidden) with the resident family. They reward well-behaved children with great gifts, but punish those who are lazy or disobedient. Either way, goblins don't like the grown-ups one bit, and take delight in making a mess of their neat kitchens.

11. Gwragged Annwn

This exquisite creature with the difficult name is the Lake Fairy in the far-away country of Wales. She has beautiful long golden hair and—despite her watery home—*no* fish tail. As you can see for yourself, she is very gentle and loves all animals, especially exotic birds.

12. Befana

Befana is a good house-fairy from Italy. She looks like a kindly old grandmother and loves little children. She brings them toys and sweets on Twelfth Night, the January holiday that marks the end of the medieval Christmas holiday. Gentle Befana even cures little ones who are not feeling well.

13. Djinn

Arabian tales have given us the words *djinn, jinni,* and *genii*—all variations of the familiar name *genie*—a powerful spirit or demon who can fulfill all wishes, bringing incredible wealth to the person who rules the spirit. The most famous *djinn* we know appears in the wondrous story of Aladdin and his magic lamp.

14. Rusalka

Rusalka is another freshwater spirit in the form of a beautiful young maiden with long golden hair. She loves to dance in the moonlight, sometimes followed by smaller spirits who help her to dress and adorn herself with flowers. One folk tale about Rusalka is almost identical to Hans Christian Andersen's familiar story, "The Little Mermaid."

15. Elves

Elves are wood spirits who look like tiny human beings. But they can also assume different forms, and are well known for misbehaving. In certain lands they were thought to cause diseases in humans and cattle. They've even been accused of sitting upon the breast of a sleeping person, to give him bad dreams. This one is about to ride a friendly rabbit like a horse!

16. Lorelei

Stories about this lovely siren come from Germany. They tell us how she sits close to dangerous rapids, and with irresistible singing lures unwary sailors into those treacherous waters. A famous statue of Lorelei is still found on the river Rhine, where she lures thousands of enchanted tourists to this day.

17. Gremlins

Gremlins—who look like rabbits with human expressions—have been blamed for every unexplainable problem one can imagine! Their misbehavior was first described at the end of World War II by British pilots who blamed gremlins for such unexpected troubles as a propellor that stopped turning all by itself! But gremlins usually made up for their mischief by helping damaged planes return home.

18. Apsaras

Apsaras are very beautiful female spirits of nature whose stories come to us from Hindu mythology. Usually water nymphs or mythical creatures of the forest, they are associated with spirits of air and music. They are graceful dancers who inspire lovers and often perform for gods.

19. Gnomes

Gnomes are like little dwarfs living underground in small houses. Down there, hidden deep below the land, they hide incredible treasures in their own small mines. Gnomes possess many powers and can disappear at will—*just like that!!*

20. Brownies

In the whole wide world of magical creatures, the brownie is the best household spirit you could ever wish for! As helpful as can be, there's nothing he won't do for a family. In return, he asks for nothing more than a dish of the best cream and a piece of freshly baked bread. (Don't offer him more, or he'll be insulted and will run away.)

21. Gum Nut Babies

These adorable, gentle fairy children are everywhere in nature, full of mischief but they hurt nothing for they love all the world. They help baby birds to fly, care for the little ones if the parents are away, and even race with the fish under-water. Australian writer May Gibbs was the first to tell us all about Gum Nut Babies, 'way back in 1915.

22. Korrigan

Stories of these beautiful maidens come to us from the folklore of northern France. This creature is seen here riding a handsome stallion—her favorite male companion. But after a long night of dancing, these maidens would magically transform themselves into old hags. What a strange sight that would be!

23. Klaboterman

This sturdy little fellow looks like he knows his way around ships and the sea—
and indeed he does. He's a spirit from the distant Baltic Sea, those cold waters
that wash the shores of Scandanavia. There, Klaboterman uses his skills in nav-
igating ships to help sea-going folks in trouble on the vast open waters.

24. Hobgoblins

As you can see, the hobgoblin looks like an ugly small elf. Depite his ferocious appearance, this creature usually helps humans with their farm chores—that is, when he's not doing his favorite sport . . . riding a farm animal as if it were a horse.

25. Leprechauns

The leprechaun is fairyland's official shoemaker. It's said that you can find him by following the tapping sound of his little silver hammer as he helps fairies with their footwear. And if you ever catch him, he must give you either his pot of gold or three magical wishes. But he can vanish in the blink of an eye—so don't get tricked by this clever fellow!

26. Mab

Empress of Fairies, Mab lives underground in a wondrous palace made of gemstones and precious metals, surrounded by an eternal garden of exquisite flowers forever in full bloom. She is so tiny that she can ride in a magical coach drawn by three butterflies.

27. Maui

Raised by the sea gods and taught by the Sky, the Great Spirit Maui is responsible for many creative activities—separating earth from sky . . . capturing the sun and regulating its movements . . . bringing fire to man . . . and, in a great act of creation, drawing up earth from the bottom of the Pacific Ocean to create the Hawaiian Islands. With leis around his neck and blossoms adorning his head, Maui is shown here shaping his beloved islands—including the one named for him.

28. Water Babies

Native North Americans believe that these lively spirits of the woodlands forever protect freshwater springs, streams, and rivers of their land. Sometimes these creatures take the shape of tiny old folks, sometimes (as we see here) as a warrior in full dress. To protect their stock of fishes, these spirits love to play tricks on fishermen.

29. Pixies

The lore of the pixie was born among the ancient Celtic folk of England's Cornwall. Tiny, with large pointed ears, narrow green eyes, and a turned-up nose, these "little folk" traditionally wore green garments to blend in with the pastures about them. Today's pixies are said to have butterfly wings, wear tiny bells to accompany their dancing, favor the moon at midnight, and dance till dawn. (It's also said that if you awake to find your horse in a lather, you can be sure that a mischievous pixie has ridden that horse all night long!)